SANCTUARY

Susan Louise Roberts
Illustrated by Aletha Heyman

To Alec &
Casey,
Woof!
Woof!
Woof!
Susan
Roberts

Abandoned and lonely,

the

BIG BROWN DOG

wandered through the

WILD WOODS.

He was hoping to find a

friend and a safe home.

"WOOF!"

he barked to the scampering chipmunk, its cheeks round with acorns.

"WOOF!"

he barked to the woodpecker which rat-a-tat-tatted on the ancient tree trunk.

"WOOF!

he barked to the snake which slithered through the fallen leaves.

But all of the forest creatures ignored him.

The big brown dog followed his nose out of the woods into a meadow, still hoping to find a **friend and a safe home.**

"WOOF!"

he barked to the butterfly as it swooped amongst the milk thistles.

"WOOF!"

he barked to the bumblebee as it danced and buzzed from flower to flower.

"WOOF!

he barked to the swallow which darted and dove through the washed blue sky.

But, like the forest creatures, all of the meadow creatures ignored him too.

Once again, the **big brown dog** followed his nose. This time he came out of the meadow at a farmhouse, still hoping to find a **friend and a safe home.**

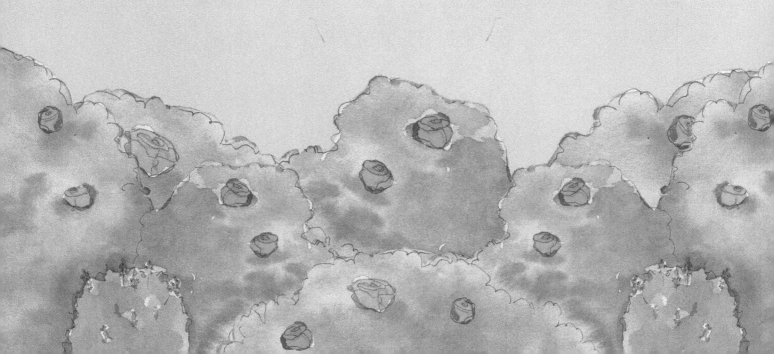

"**WOOF!**"

he barked to the lady who smiled and kneeled to greet him.

"**WELL, HELLO,**" she said.

"**WOOF!**"

he barked again, this time wagging his tail.

The lady gazed at the
old brown Labrador retriever.

"What a sweet boy you are. My name is

RUTHIE."

She noticed that he wasn't wearing
a collar. His fur was dirty, and he was
too skinny for a dog his size.

The **big brown dog**
sat patiently in front of her.

He cocked his head this way and that,
looking at **RUTHIE** with soft
soulful eyes.

RUTHIE wondered where the dog had come from and how he had found his way to her wilderness sanctuary.

She knew he couldn't tell her his story, but she wondered if she could guess his name.

First she said the long vowel sounds of A, E, I, O and U, saying the words,

"APE, EAR, ICE, OPEN, UNICORN."

Sitting, the big brown dog just looked at her.

Next she tried the **short vowel** sounds of
A, E, I, O and U,
saying,

"APPLE,
ELEPHANT,
IGUANA,
OTTER,
UMBRELLA."

The **big brown dog** lay down, still looking at her.

Next Ruthie rounded her mouth and made the long 'OO' sound saying, "FOOD."

Suddenly, the big brown dog stood up and barked, "WOOF!"

Ruthie laughed and started to add consonants to the long 'OO' sound saying, "BOO, DO, POO."

The big brown dog barked softly, "woof."

"*Hmm,*" Ruthie thought, trying again saying, "COO, MOO, LOU."

"WOOF!   WOOF!   WOOF!"

"Well, well, well," Ruthie chuckled. "I guess your name is LOU."

RUTHIE gently stroked

LOU'S large brown head.

He followed her, and his nose,
into her cozy home.

Later that night, with his stomach full and his coat brushed, **LOU** lay comfortably at **RUTHIE'S** feet.

The next day, RUTHIE called the animal rescue to ask if anyone was looking for a missing brown retriever dog.

The answer was no. So RUTHIE, with a happy heart, adopted LOU.

LOU finally had a friend and a safe home with RUTHIE at the

WILDERNESS SANCTUARY.

WOOF!

GUIDING QUESTIONS

1. What is the story SANCTUARY about?

2. Why do you think Ruthie wants to guess Lou's name rather than give him a new one?

3. Do you think names are important? Why or why not?

4. Tell something special about your name.

5. Let's find the vowel and consonants in your name!

6. How does Lou change from the beginning of the story to the end of the story?

7. What kind of person is Ruthie? What character traits does she have?

8. Write or tell or draw a story about an adventure that Lou and Ruthie might have at the Wilderness Sanctuary.

9. What are animal shelters/rescues? Let's talk about their purpose in our communities, and the types of animals you might find at a shelter.

10. Sometimes people need sanctuary too. Let's talk about that.

Dedicated to my grandchildren,
Cora and Bobby

Thank you for purchasing *Sanctuary*.
A portion of the proceeds from the sale of
the book directly support:

Creation of Hope's "Rolling Hills Residence"
which offers support, a home and education
to orphans and vulnerable children
in the small town of Kikima, Mbooni
Region, Kenya
@hopestory.ca

Kingston Animal Rescue:
www. kingstonanimalrescue.com

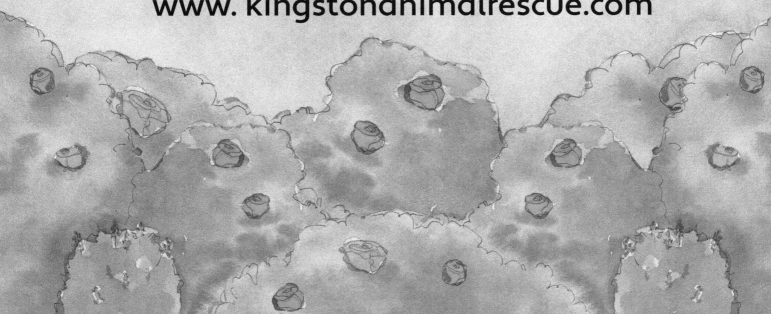

Ruthie and Lou – Adoption Day
Photo used with permission
www.borealexperiences.com

Children at play.
Rolling Hills Residence (2019)
Photo used with permission @hopestory.ca

FriesenPress

One Printers Way
Altona, MB R0G 0B0
Canada

www.friesenpress.com

Copyright © 2022 Susan Louise Roberts
First Edition — 2022

Illustrated by Aletha Heyman

ISBN
978-1-03-912640-4 (Hardcover)
978-1-03-912639-8 (Paperback)
978-1-03-912641-1 (eBook)

1. JUVENILE FICTION, SOCIAL ISSUES, FRIENDSHIP

Distributed to the trade by The Ingram Book Company

CPSIA information can be obtained
at www.ICGtesting.com
Printed in the USA
BVHW022148191122
651042BV00005B/12